Illustrated by
Nicoletta Oeccoli

Based upon the story
by Hans Christian Andersen

 **McGraw-Hill**
Children's Publishing

McGraw-Hill
Children's Publishing

A Division of The **McGraw·Hill** Companies

This edition published in the United States in 2002 by
McGraw-Hill Children's Publishing,
A Division of The McGraw-Hill Companies
8787 Orion Place
Columbus, Ohio 43240

www.MHkids.com

ISBN 1-58845-478-9

Library of Congress Cataloging-in-Publication Data is on file with the publisher.

10 9 8 7 6 5 4 3 2 1 CHRT 06 05 04 03 02

Printed in China.

Thumbelina

Illustrated by

Nicoletta Oeccoli

Once upon a time, there lived a kind woman whose fondest wish was to have a daughter. So she went to visit a wise, old witch who gave her a magic coffee bean.

"Now deary," said the witch. "Take this bean home and plant it in a pot. Give it plenty of sun and water. Be patient and loving, and your wish will come true."

A few days later, a beautiful flower sprouted in the pot. The woman was so enchanted with the lovely flower that she bent down to kiss its soft petals. Suddenly, the flower opened and the woman found a precious little girl inside, no bigger than her thumb. The woman named her Thumbelina.

The woman loved Thumbelina very much. She made a soft, cozy bed for her out of a walnut shell and filled a soup bowl with water so Thumbelina would have her own small lake to play in.

One night, an ugly toad passed by Thumbelina's window and saw the girl fast asleep in her walnut shell bed.

"She will make a perfect wife for my son!" said the toad, and he stole Thumbelina away.

The toad brought Thumbelina to his home by the river and introduced her to his short, warty son and his plump, warty wife. He placed the girl on a lily pad where she could not escape.

"Are you pleased with your new bride, my son?" asked the toad. "Croak!" said his son. He was very pleased and thought Thumbelina was quite pretty, even though she wasn't green.

Thumbelina thought of the kind woman who had made her a walnut shell bed, and she began to cry.

A fish swimming by heard Thumbelina's sobs. He felt sorry for her and nibbled at the stem of the lily pad where she sat, until it broke free.

"Oh, thank you!" called Thumbelina.

Thumbelina drifted down the river, away from the toad and his son.
She sailed past villages and towns. She gazed at the wide blue sky above
her and watched seagulls soaring through the air. *To be as free as a bird
must be a marvelous thing*, she thought.

Just then, a beetle flying over the sparkling river saw Thumbelina floating on the water below. Thinking her very beautiful, the beetle plucked Thumbelina from the lily pad and carried her to the top of a tree.

The beetle was very proud of his new little treasure. He went to visit the other beetles and bugs so he could present Thumbelina to them. But the other beetles did not find Thumbelina lovely at all! They thought she was a very strange-looking creature and laughed so much that the beetle was very embarrassed.

He decided that Thumbelina was not such a treasure after all and let her go free.

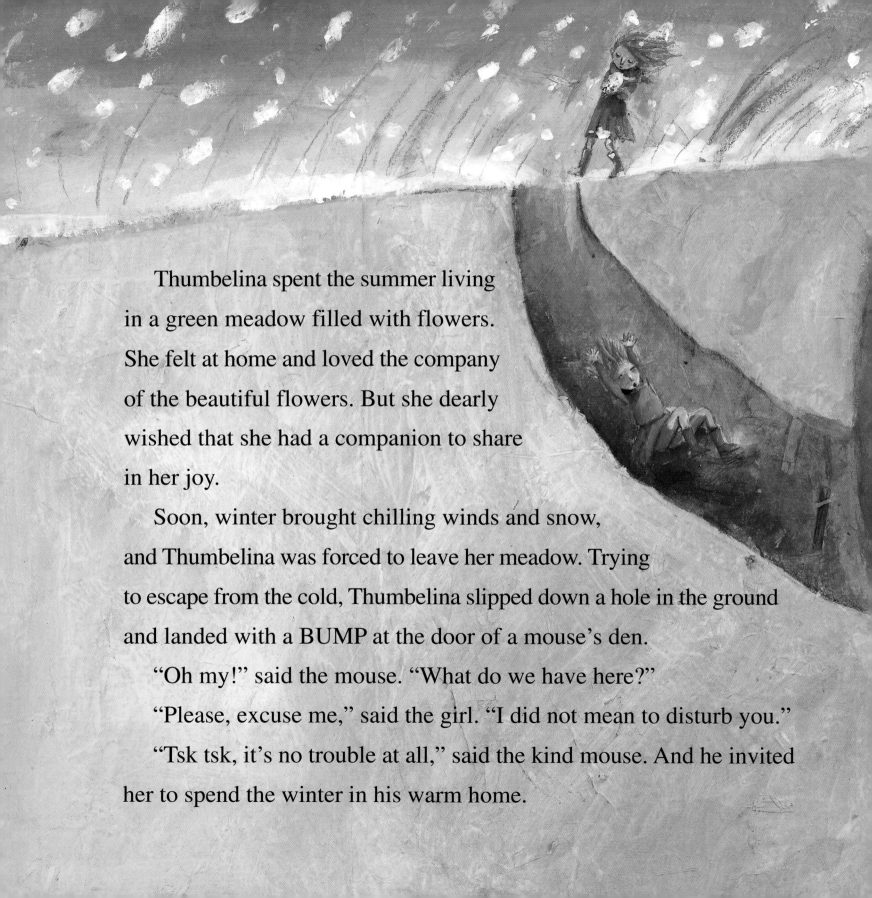

Thumbelina spent the summer living
in a green meadow filled with flowers.
She felt at home and loved the company
of the beautiful flowers. But she dearly
wished that she had a companion to share
in her joy.

Soon, winter brought chilling winds and snow,
and Thumbelina was forced to leave her meadow. Trying
to escape from the cold, Thumbelina slipped down a hole in the ground
and landed with a BUMP at the door of a mouse's den.

"Oh my!" said the mouse. "What do we have here?"

"Please, excuse me," said the girl. "I did not mean to disturb you."

"Tsk tsk, it's no trouble at all," said the kind mouse. And he invited
her to spend the winter in his warm home.

Thumbelina and the mouse passed a few pleasant weeks in the cozy den. The mouse gave Thumbelina a snug bed and delicious food. In turn, she kept his house neat for him.

One day Mr. Mole dropped in for a visit. "What a pretty little girl you have staying with you, my friend," said the mole. "And look how tidy and neat your den has become since she came to visit!"

Mr. Mole thought about his own lonely den and how very nice it would be to have Thumbelina take care of him.

"I believe that I have lived alone too long, my friend," said Mr. Mole. "I am ready to take a wife, and Thumbelina would make a sweet bride."

The mouse, who was very fond of both Thumbelina and Mr. Mole, thought this was a wonderful idea.

And Thumbelina, who did not wish to offend the kind mouse, agreed to the marriage.

However, the thought of living underground for the rest of her days saddened her very much.

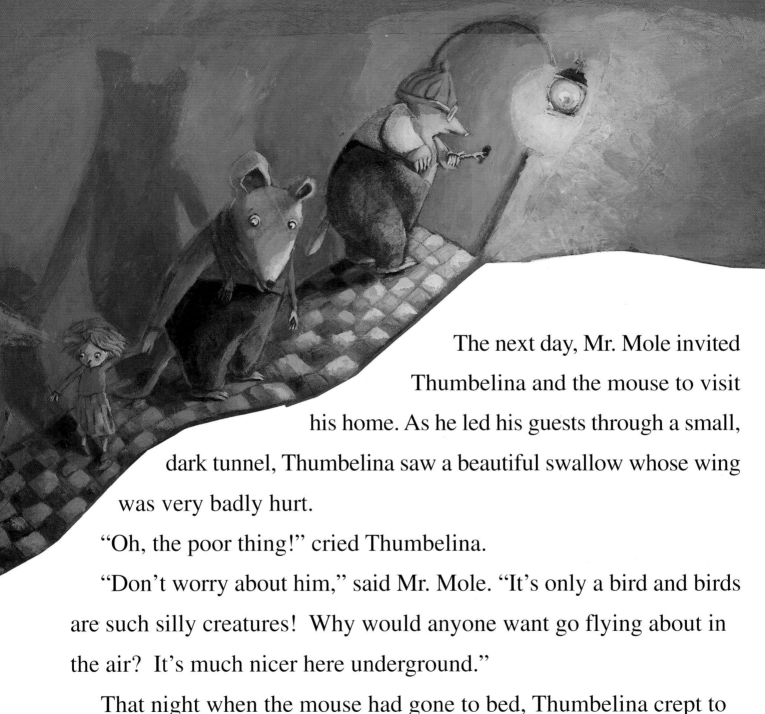

The next day, Mr. Mole invited Thumbelina and the mouse to visit his home. As he led his guests through a small, dark tunnel, Thumbelina saw a beautiful swallow whose wing was very badly hurt.

"Oh, the poor thing!" cried Thumbelina.

"Don't worry about him," said Mr. Mole. "It's only a bird and birds are such silly creatures! Why would anyone want go flying about in the air? It's much nicer here underground."

That night when the mouse had gone to bed, Thumbelina crept to the spot where she had seen the swallow and covered him with a soft blanket.

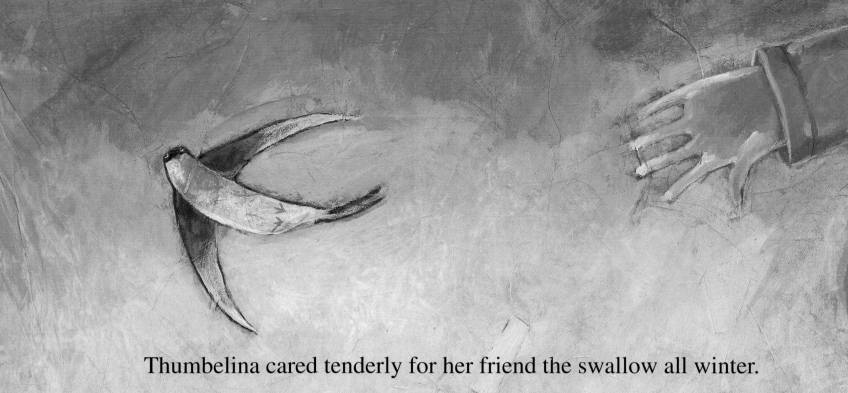

Thumbelina cared tenderly for her friend the swallow all winter.

In the spring, the swallow was well enough to leave the tunnel and return to his home in the sky. Thumbelina snuck outside and set the swallow free.

"Good-bye, my little friend," said the swallow. "Perhaps we will meet again."

"Good-bye, my dear swallow," said Thumbelina sadly.

She was sorry to see her friend go and wished she could fly away with him, leaving Mr. Mole and his dark, narrow tunnel behind her forever.

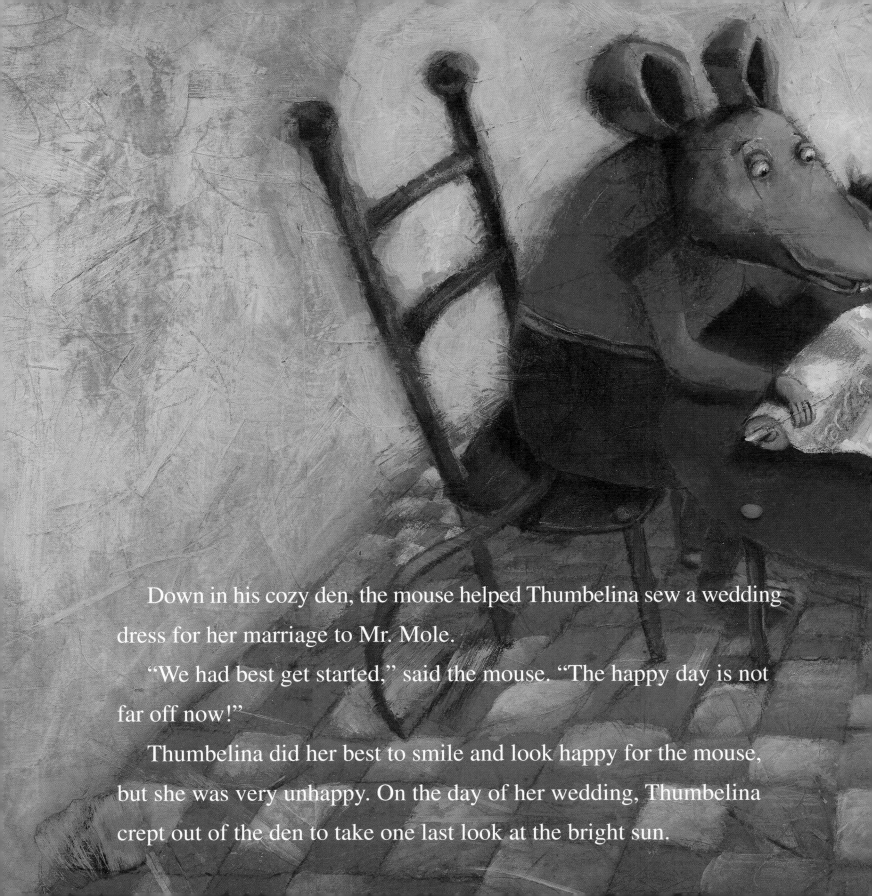

Down in his cozy den, the mouse helped Thumbelina sew a wedding dress for her marriage to Mr. Mole.

"We had best get started," said the mouse. "The happy day is not far off now!"

Thumbelina did her best to smile and look happy for the mouse, but she was very unhappy. On the day of her wedding, Thumbelina crept out of the den to take one last look at the bright sun.

As she stood looking at the sky and breathing
in the fresh, clean air one last time, Thumbelina
heard a familiar voice. It was her friend the swallow!
"Come along, Thumbelina," said the swallow. "Climb onto
my back and I will take you away from here."
"Oh my dear friend," cried Thumbelina. "You have
not forgotten me!"
Together they flew high into the sky, then away towards
a beautiful meadow where the swallow had his nest.
Flying free as a bird was indeed a marvelous thing!

The swallow set Thumbelina down in the middle of a bright flower. Standing on the flower beside her, Thumbelina saw a handsome young man, who smiled warmly at Thumbelina and took her hand.

"I am the Flower King," said the young man. "I look after and protect all the flower folk who live in this meadow. I welcome you to my kingdom and I hope you will be happy here."

Thumbelina, the little girl born in a flower, had finally found
a place where she belonged. Over time, Thumbelina and the
Flower King became very fond of each other. They
fell in love and were married. And there among
the flowers, they lived happily ever after.

The End